Jean Abernethy Presents

Fergus

and
The Night Before Christmas

TS
TRAFALGAR SQUARE
North Pomfret, Vermont

First published in 2018 by
Trafalgar Square Books
North Pomfret, Vermont 05053

Copyright © 2018 Jean Abernethy

Trafalgar Square Books encourages the use of approved safety helmets in all equestrian sports and activities.

Library of Congress Cataloging-in-Publication Data
Names: Abernethy, Jean, author, illustrator.
Title: Fergus and the night before Christmas / Jean Abernethy.
Description: North Pomfret, Vermont : Trafalgar Square Books, 2018. |
  Summary: On Christmas Eve, Fergus the cartoon horse leads a noisy and
  mismatched team to draw Santa's sleigh and deliver a special present in
  this take-off on the classic poem.
Identifiers: LCCN 2018019734 | ISBN 9781570768965 (hardcover)
Subjects: | CYAC: Stories in rhyme. | Horses--Fiction. | Christmas--Fiction.
  | Santa Claus--Fiction. | Humorous stories.
Classification: LCC PZ8.3.A1285 Fer 2018 | DDC [E]--dc23
LC record available at https://lccn.loc.gov/2018019734

Book and cover design by RM Didier
Typefaces: Harrington, Verdana

Printed in China

10 9 8 7 6 5 4 3

For Mom & Dad

'Twas the night before Christmas,
the sky, dark as ink,
and I couldn't sleep,
no, not even a wink!

No visions of sugar plums,
        like the rhyme says.
I don't even know what a sugar plum is!

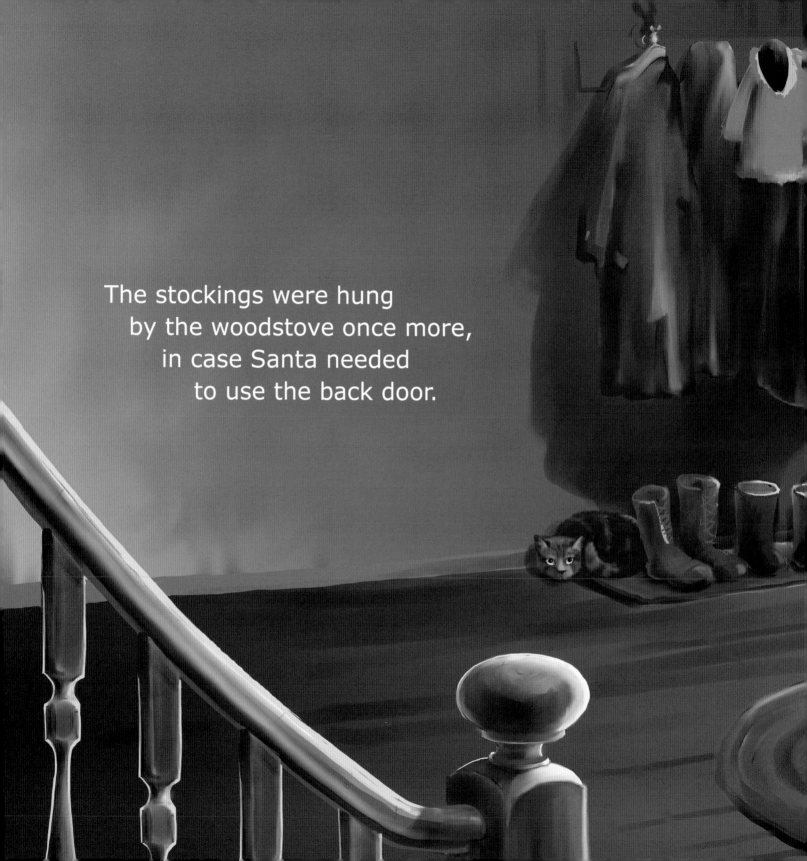

The stockings were hung
   by the woodstove once more,
   in case Santa needed
      to use the back door.

I was snuggled in bed
    with my heart all a-tingle,
        when somewhere outside
            came a ring and a jingle!

I jumped up to look for
            eight tiny reindeer,
    with my face on the window
(my nose made a smear).

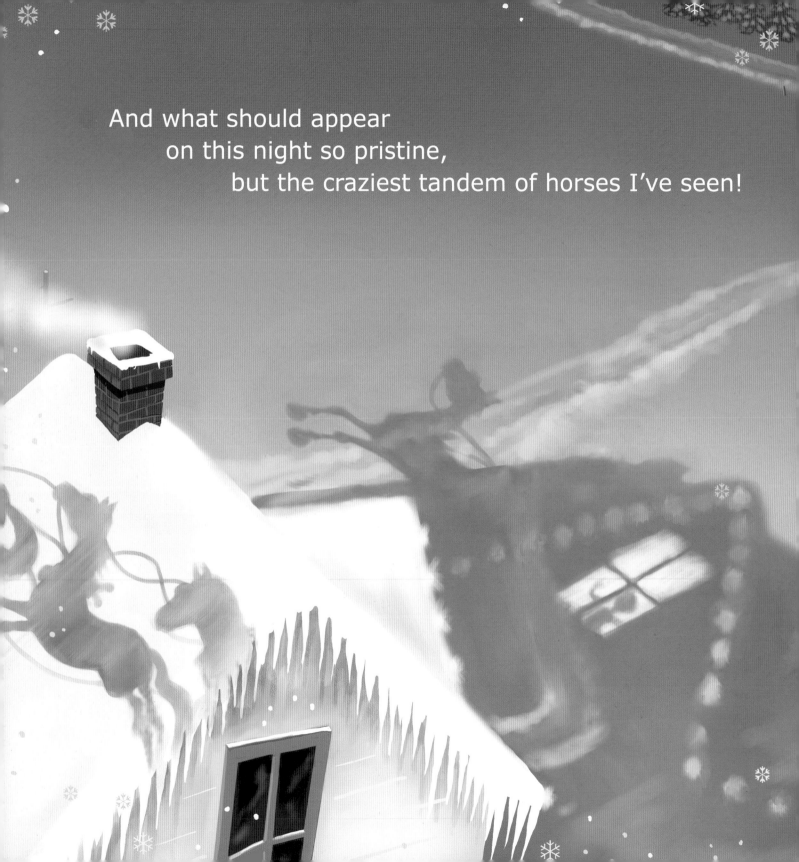

And what should appear
 on this night so pristine,
  but the craziest tandem of horses I've seen!

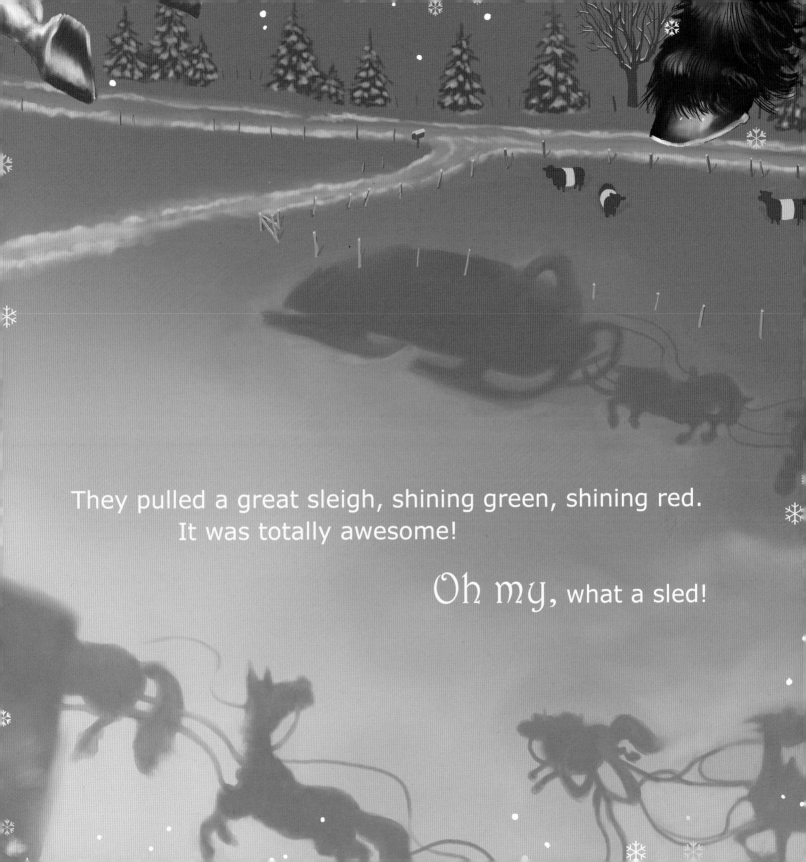

They pulled a great sleigh, shining green, shining red.
It was totally awesome!

Oh my, what a sled!

The harness, it sparkled,
    and jingled and jangled
with buckles and bells,
    all nicely fandangled.

I counted them out
    as they soared through the heavens.
Instead of eight horses,
    they numbered eleven!

With a snowy-faced leader
        so spooky and quick,
I started to worry
        about old St. Nick!

This horse had ONe shoe,
        and a little hay belly,
and googley eyes
        that were utterly silly.

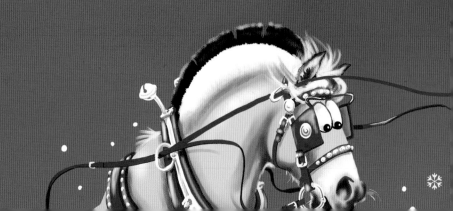

I surely love horses, but this was a fright!
A truly fantastic, ridiculous sight!

The whole team a mismatch of color and size.
That Santa could drive them
was the biggest surprise!

But drive them he did!
    To his leader did shout,
        "Easy there, Fergus,
                don't make me fall out!"

His eyes didn't twinkle.
    His dimples weren't merry.
            The look on his face was a little bit scary!

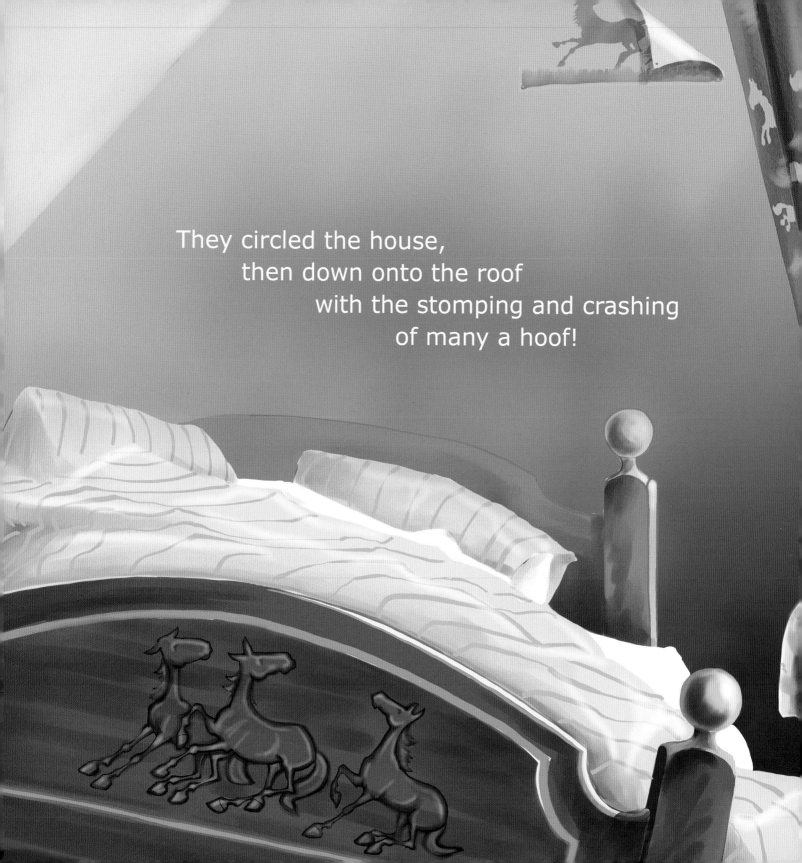

They circled the house,
        then down onto the roof
                with the stomping and crashing
                        of many a hoof!

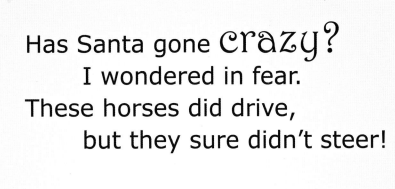

Has Santa gone crazy?
        I wondered in fear.
These horses did drive,
        but they sure didn't steer!

They clung to the gables,
        they hung from the eaves,
and spread o'er the garden
        like fresh autumn leaves.

As I stared, dumbfounded,
at this sorry lot,
I saw something,
possibly,
Santa *did not*.

The one he called Fergus
        (the leader, of course)
                made his way back to the littlest horse.

She squirmed and she giggled and wiggled, as he...

...unbuckled her harness...

...and let her go free.

She shuffled away,
and was soon out of sight.
Had something gone wrong
on their Christmas Eve flight?

She'd simply
abandoned
her teammates!

What's more...

...she'd stolen the Christmas wreath
off our front door!

I started to fret,
to worry and ponder.
Where was she going?
How far would she wander?

Could Santa continue without his whole team?
Had Fergus been plotting some terrible scheme?

If St. Nick was stuck on our roof with his load,
how would he get to the kids down the road?

Was Pony just hungry...or running away?
Or trying to get back to Santa's big sleigh?

I stuck to the windowpane, wondering whether
Santa could put that whole mess back together.

A few little presents
　　　lay out in the snow.
But what of the stockings
　　　that hung down below?

With a shudder, some dust
　　　and some drywall came down,
as St. Nick took the lines,
　　　and he turned them for town.

The sleigh gave a groan,
　　　and the roof did the same,
as he whistled and shouted
　　　and called them by name.

"Monique! Hughie! Hup!
Bring on the muscle!"

"On Clevis, on Dottie!
   Look lively there, Russell!
Listen up, Fergus!
Step into it, Art!"

And the whole team took off
     with a buck and a fart.

"Lean into your collars,
Bjorn and dear Kase!
We're headin' for Cleveland, Ray...

...Hey! Where is Grace?"

I froze in my slippers,
just watching them go
with one empty harness
that dangled below.

I supposed as I viewed
that incredible team
    that it's cool for a small kid
        to have a big dream.

'Cause as they flew into
the sky dark as ink
    I'm sure I saw Fergus
        look back and wink.

MERRY CHRISTMAS